The Little Drummer Boy

The boy tapped on his drum as he watched the camels drink. He wondered where the three wise men were going that starry night.

Pa-rum-pum-pum-pum, he played. The little Drummer Boy had made the drum himself from animal skin and a piece of an old hollow log. *Rum-pum-pum-pum*. To his ears, his music on the drum sounded like the sound the camels made as they drank.

Finally the three wise men came out, their robes trailing behind them. "Are the camels ready?" asked the first.

The boy hid his drum behind his back. He didn't want them to think he wasn't doing his job. "They are ready, Sirs," he said.

"It's a fine night for a journey," said the second wise man.

The Drummer Boy could stand it no longer. "Tell me!" he pleaded. "Where are you going?"

"We're following that star," said the third wise man, pointing to the brightest star in the sky.

The Drummer Boy watched them load a heavy box of gold onto the first camel. Next came a jar of fragrant frankincense, then precious myrrh.

"Why do you carry gifts?" asked the Drummer Boy.

"The star will lead us to the newborn King," said the first wise man.

"Please, let me come with you," begged the Drummer Boy. And the wise men agreed.

The Drummer Boy fell in behind the three wise men. As the camels' hooves went clippity-clop, the boy played his drum: *Rat-tat-ta-tat*. He was on his way to see the newborn King.

Suddenly the Drummer Boy had a terrible thought! He wanted to give something wonderful to the child, but he had nothing to give. He owned nothing that could please a king.

Day after day they traveled on. The Drummer Boy kept the camels moving with his steady drumming: *Da-da-drum-drum.*

The star led them all the way to Bethlehem to a manger. The three wise men knelt before the baby and presented their gifts of gold, frankincense, and myrrh.

But the little Drummer Boy waited outside. How could he go in without a gift?

Suddenly the Drummer Boy heard
a cry. He peeked into the stable. The
sheep pushed at their stall. Oxen
pawed the ground. Donkeys brayed.
And the baby cried.

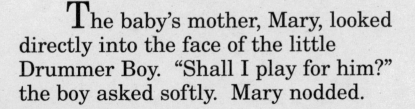

The baby's mother, Mary, looked directly into the face of the little Drummer Boy. "Shall I play for him?" the boy asked softly. Mary nodded.

Slowly the Drummer Boy began to play. *Pa-rum-pum-pum-pum.* The ox and lambs kept time. *Pa-rum-pum-pum-pum.*

The Drummer Boy drew nearer to Baby Jesus. 'I'll play my best for him,' he thought. *Pa-rum-pum-pum-pum. Rum-pum-pum-pum, Rum-pum-pum-pum.* On his drum.

By the time the Drummer Boy finished, Baby Jesus had stopped crying. The little Drummer Boy gently lay down his drum beside the manger. And when he looked in, he was sure the newborn King's smile was just for him.